The Pigeon Finds a Hot Dog!

For Cheryl

ISBN 0-439-80012-9

Text and illustrations © 2004 by Mo Willems. All rights reserved.
Published by Scholastic Inc., 557 Broadway, New York, NY 10012, by arrangement with
Hyperion Books for Children, an imprint of Disney Children's Book Group, LLC.
SCHOLASTIC and associated logos are trademarks and/or registered trademarks of Scholastic Inc.

12 11 10 9 8 7 6 5 4 3 2 1   5 6 7 8 9 10/0

Printed in the U.S.A.   40

First Scholastic printing, October 2005

The Pigeon Finds a Hot Dog!

words and pictures by mo willems

SCHOLASTIC INC.

New York Toronto London Auckland Sydney
Mexico City New Delhi Hong Kong Buenos Aires

I have a
question.

Of course!
Enjoy!

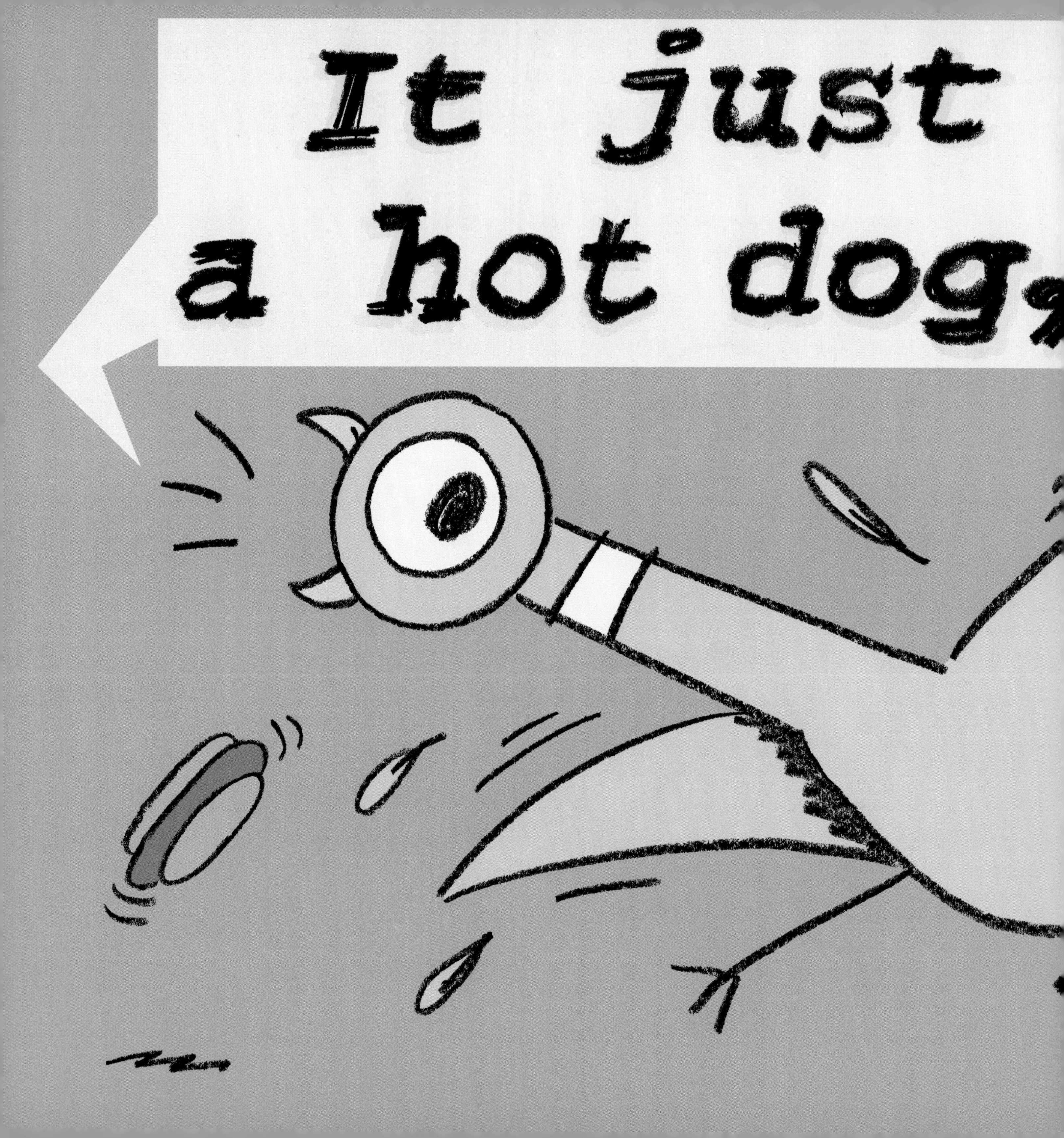
It just
a hot dog,

tastes like okay!?

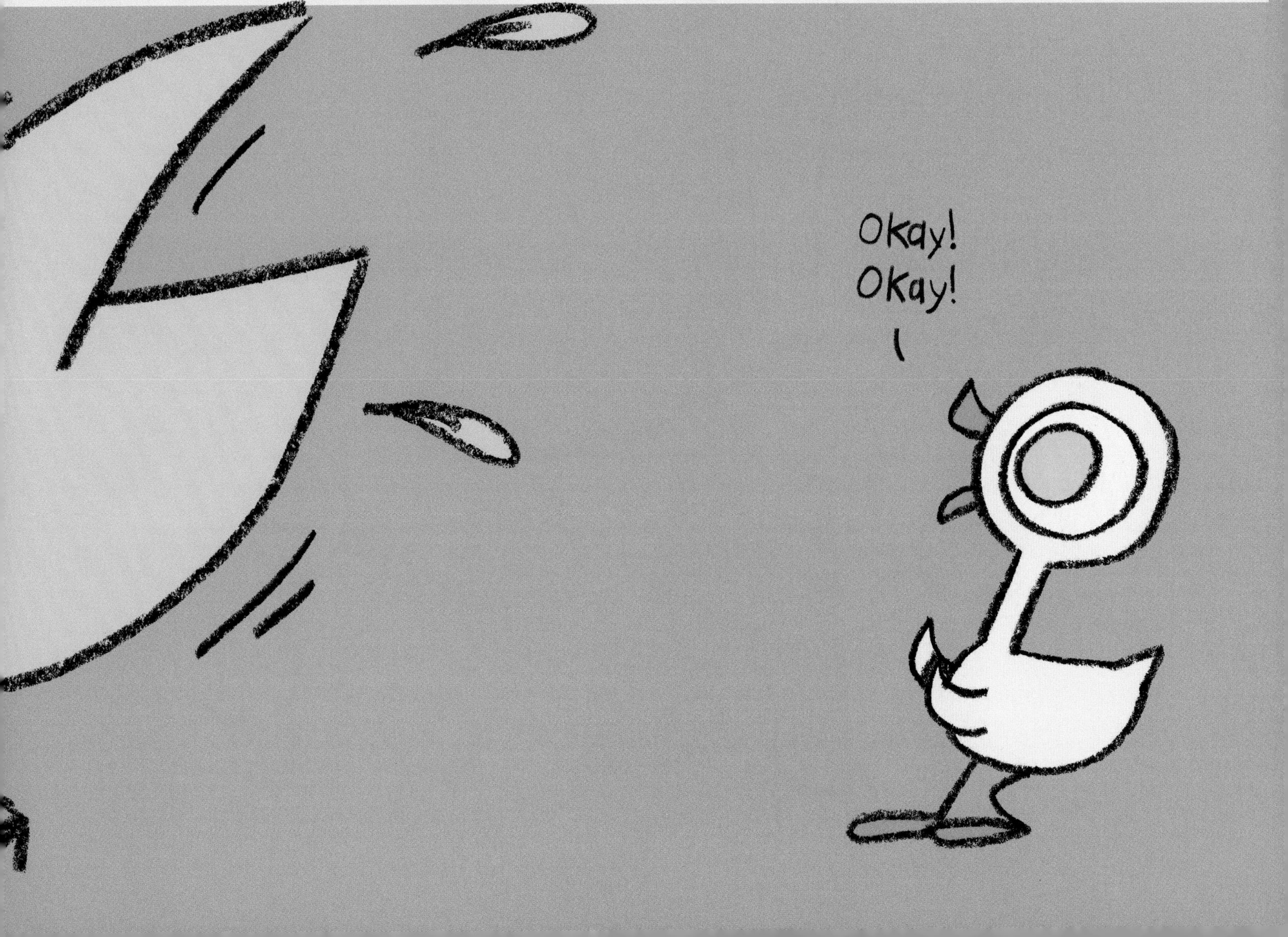

So, it doesn't
taste like
chicken, then?

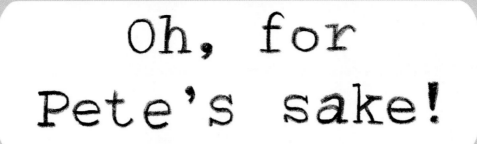

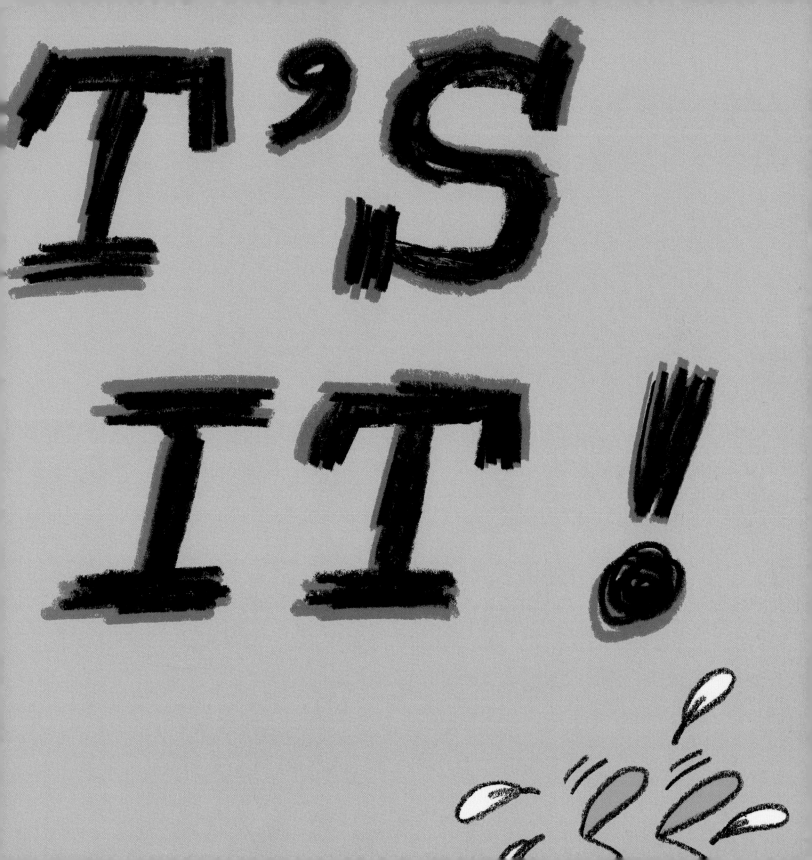

You know, you're pretty smart for a duckling.

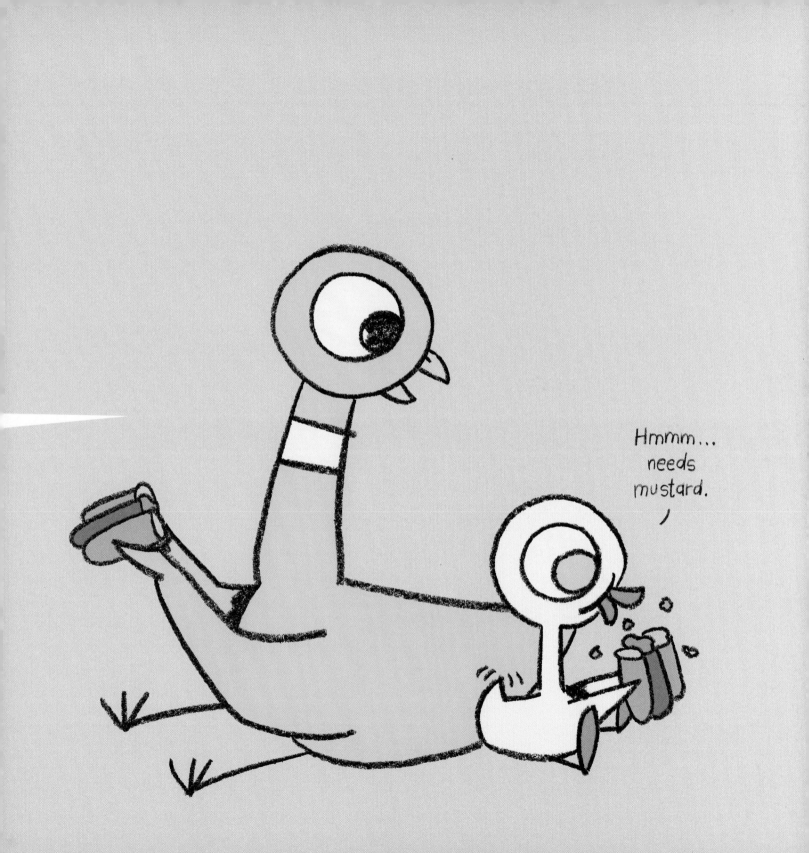

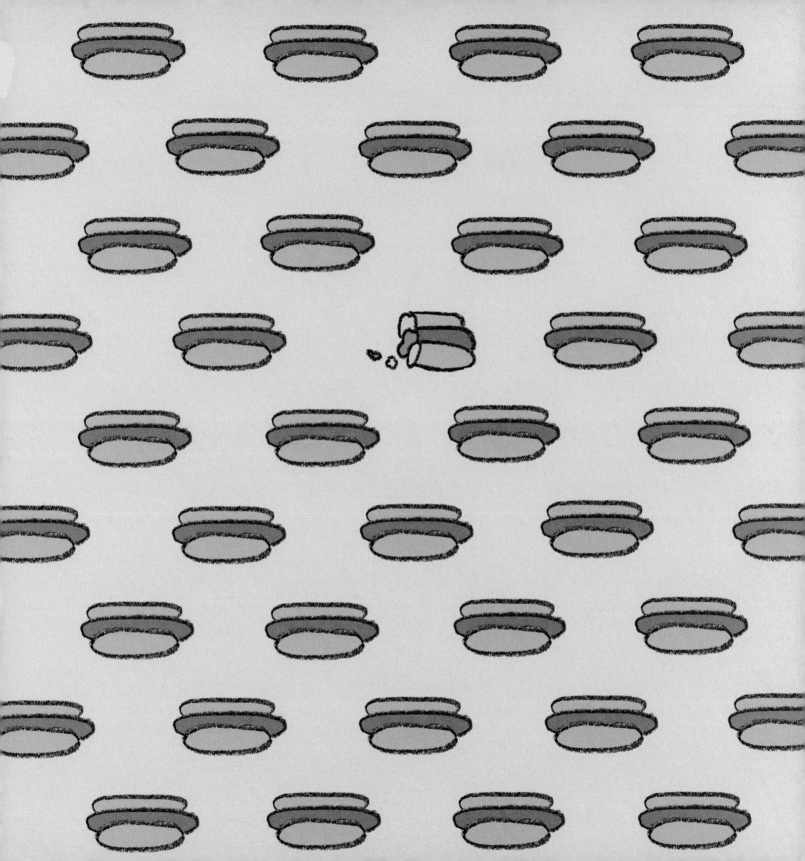